Sarah Weeks

GUY WIRE

SCHOLASTIC INC.

New York Toronto London Auckland Sydney
Mexico City New Delhi Hong Kong Buenos Aires

ISBN 0-439-56214-7

12 11 10 9 8 7 6 5 4 3 2   3 4 5 6 7 8/0

Printed in the U.S.A.   40

First Scholastic printing, September 2003

GUY WIRE

sld

—S.W.

Chapter One

"You know what I've been thinking about lately?" I said to Buzz as we rode our bikes down the street toward my house one afternoon during spring break.

"What to give me for my birthday tomorrow?" he said.

"No. I've been thinking about fate."

"What's fate?" asked Buzz, licking his palm and trying to plaster down the hair sticking up at the back of his head. He has a bunch of cowlicks, which make his hair stand up funny sometimes.

"Fate is like when stuff happens out of the blue and you can't really explain why," I said.

"You mean like belching?" Buzz asked.

"No, you gall bladder, like getting hit by lightning. Or happening to meet the person you're going to get married to while you're standing in line at the grocery store minding your own business."

"I'm never going to get married," said Buzz.

"You don't know that," I said. "For all you know, fate has her all picked out for you already. The future Mrs. Buzz Adams could be walking around Cedar Springs right now."

"Sheesh, Guy. That's creepy. You mean, even if I don't want to get married, I have to because of this fate thing?"

"You can't fight fate," I said. "It's a losing battle."

"If we actually do have to get married someday, do you think either one of us is gonna have a wedding like the one your mom had?" Buzz asked. "Remember that?"

"*Remember* it?" I snorted. "Are you kidding? She wore a dress made out of Styrofoam cups, and the groom played the wedding march on a hose nozzle. Who could forget something like that?"

My parents are divorced, and my mom got remarried last Valentine's Day. The ceremony, like most things my mother masterminds, was a bit unusual, to put it mildly.

"The thing about marriage is I think it's sort of like rolling dice. Everybody wants to roll a six and live happily ever after. But if it turns out you roll a four, then you've got to decide whether to stick with that or take a chance on rolling again," I said. "Sure, maybe you'll get lucky and roll a six the second time around, but then again you could end up rolling a two and be worse off than when you started."

"Are the dice real ones, or fuzzy ones?" Buzz asked seriously.

"What difference does that make?"

"Real ones roll better than fuzzy ones," he explained simply.

I stopped pedaling and looked at him.

"Why do you say stuff like that, Buzzard?"

"Like what?" he said.

"Like 'Real ones roll better than fuzzy ones.'"

"What's the matter with that? It's true, isn't it? Think about it, Guy. Fuzzy things don't roll very well. Take rabbits, for instance. It'd be hard to roll a rabbit, don't you think?"

We both lifted ourselves up off our seats, standing on the pedals in order to put our weight into an uphill climb.

"Do you ever actually listen to yourself when you talk? You say crazy junk like that as if it's normal. Nobody rolls rabbits," I said.

"There you go," said Buzz in a self-satisfied tone. "You just proved my point. The reason nobody rolls rabbits is because they're too fuzzy. Am I right, or am I right?"

"You're nuts is what you are," I said.

The next hill was too steep to ride up, so we got off our bikes and walked them next to each other.

"Do you still make a wish when you blow out the candles on your birthday cake?" Buzz asked me.

"Of course I do," I said. "Who doesn't?"

"Personally, I'm thinking about giving it up this year," he announced.

"Are you serious?"

"Yeah, I think I've finally outgrown it. Like Santa Claus and the Tooth Fairy."

"Wishing isn't like Santa Claus," I said. "It's a real thing."

"Think about it, Guy Wire. Every year you're supposed to make a wish, and the deal is, if you get all the candles out in one blow it'll come true. Right?"

"Right, as long as you don't tell anybody what you wished for," I said.

"And you believe that?" said Buzz. "Come on, have you ever gotten anything you wished for?"

"Yeah, " I said. "As a matter of fact I have."

"Oh, yeah? What?" he asked.

"I can't tell you that," I said, suddenly wishing I'd kept my big mouth shut.

"Why not?"

"I just can't," I said.

"The reason you can't tell me is because it's not true. Just admit it, Guy Wire."

"No, I swear, once I really did get what I wished for. I just don't want to tell you what it was, that's all. It might be dangerous."

"Dangerous?" Buzz said.

"Yeah, like maybe telling you about it could make the wish come untrue."

"That is such bunk." Buzz snorted. "Besides, the deal is we tell each other everything. So if there really is something to tell, spill it or else."

I wasn't sure exactly why it felt wrong, I just knew it did. But for some reason I took a deep breath and told him anyway.

"I wished for you," I said.

"What are you talking about, corn dog?"

"On my seventh birthday I wished for a best friend. A few months later you moved here. So my wish came true. Okay?" We'd reached the top of the hill, so we both got on our bikes and began to pedal.

"For real?" he asked. "Did you really do

that? Wish for me?"

"I didn't exactly wish for *you*. I wished for *somebody*, and it turned out to be you," I tried to explain. "Can we please just drop it now?"

We rode in silence for a minute, and then Buzz said, "When I turned five, I wished for ballet lessons."

"Get out!" I laughed.

"Get in. I swear. There was this girl in my kindergarten class who got to leave school early three afternoons a week for ballet. Seemed like a good deal to me, so I wished for it on my birthday," Buzz said.

"Did you even know what ballet was?" I asked.

"Of course not, you drill bit. Can you see me jumping around in a tutu and tights?"

"Depends. What color is the tutu?" I asked.

Buzz reached over and grabbed my handlebars, giving them a quick jerk, which set my bike wobbling uncontrollably under me. Then he sped ahead of me, whooping and hollering.

"Last one home is a rotten egg!" he called back over his shoulder.

I regained my balance as quickly as I could and chased after him.

"That's it, gum ball. Prepare to die!" I yelled as he zipped out of sight around the corner ahead of me.

I heard it before I saw it. Screeching tires and a sickening *thunk*. And then—then—just silence. I pedaled as fast as I could, holding my breath as I rounded the corner.

"Don't let it be. Don't let it be," I whispered over and over.

But it was.

Chapter Two

"I didn't even see him. He came out of nowhere," the man said as he got out of his car and came over to where Buzz was lying in the street.

"He's not—? Is he—?" I almost didn't recognize the sound of my own voice, it was so small and pinched, like something was trying to squeeze my throat closed.

The man leaned over Buzz and touched his neck.

"He's breathing, and his pulse seems okay," he said as he took off his jacket and laid it gently over Buzz's still body. "But he's not conscious, and that's never a good thing."

Somebody must have called an ambulance. The police came too. I remember answering questions, but mostly I just sat on the ground next to Buzz, touching his arm and talking to him softly.

Then a wonderful thought came into my head. I bent close to his ear and whispered, "Okay, I get it now. I know what you're doing, you worm. You're lying there pretending to be out of it so you can pop up and scare the heck out of me, aren't you? Go ahead, Buzzard, pop up and get it over with. Make a fool out of me and then laugh your head off about it. I won't mind. I promise, really. Go ahead. Open your eyes, Buzzy. Come on, *please.*"

But he didn't pop up. And he didn't laugh. Or smile. Or open his eyes. And it was all my fault. I should never have told him about the wish.

They wouldn't let me ride in the ambulance with him. I watched them put him on a stretcher and lift him into the back. Then, when they drove off toward the hospital, I rode my bike the rest of the way home, dropped it in the driveway, and ran into the house to tell my mother what had happened.

"You boys are in luck; snicker doodles are just coming out of the oven!" my mother called as I came in the back door. "Buzzy, I made a double batch 'cause I knew you were com—"

"Mom?" I said.

My mother turned around, and her face changed the minute she laid eyes on me.

"What's wrong?" she asked, putting her potholder down on the counter and ignoring the timer when it dinged.

"It's Buzz," I said. "They just took him away in an ambulance."

"Oh, my God. Oh my God. What happened?" my mother cried.

Tears began streaming down my face. "He got hit by a car, Mom. Somebody hit Buzz."

"Is he okay, Guy?" she asked anxiously.

"I don't know," I said, and the words echoed through the new empty space that seemed to have taken over the whole left side of my chest.

My mother called Buzz's mom. She was on the phone for only a second; then she rushed around turning off the oven, getting her car keys, putting on her jacket, and writing a note for my stepfather, Jerry.

"I'm going to drive Barbara over to the hospital," she told me, starting for the door. "Buzz's dad is going to meet us there."

"I'm coming too."

"Are you sure you want to?" she asked.

I just looked at her.

"Of course you do," she said quietly.

Barbara Adams was already standing out on the curb at the bottom of our driveway. My mom's house, where I live half of the time, since she and my dad are divorced and split time with me, is right next door to Buzz's. She and Jerry bought the house when they decided to get married last spring.

Jerry's semiobnoxious daughter, Lana, also lives with us part of the time, but at the moment she was in California with her own mom.

Mrs. Adams had her purse over her shoulder, and she was wearing an apron over her dress. It was pink and frilly and said, "Kiss Me I'm Cookin'" on it. Buzz and I had gone shopping together and each bought one for our moms for Mother's Day a few years ago. My mom still wore hers too—but she had used white-out and a permanent marker to change hers so it said, "Kiss Me I'm Kooky!"

"Mom," I said, "do you think we should tell her she's still got her apron on?"

My mother looked at me and silently shook her head as Mrs. Adams opened the car door and quickly got in.

"Barbara, I'm so sorry," Mom said, reaching over and touching her shoulder.

"Lorraine, I'm not even going to let myself think . . ." Buzz's mom closed her eyes and pressed her lips together so tight that they turned white. A few seconds later she turned around, took my hand, and squeezed it. I shivered. Her fingers were like ice.

Hal Adams was waiting at the hospital when we got there. He and Buzz's mom were allowed to go in right away, but my mom and I had to wait out in the waiting room.

"Why can't we go in too?" I asked.

"Only family is allowed right now," my mother explained gently.

"Don't best friends count as family?" I asked.

My mother just patted my knee.

We sat down next to each other in a couple of gray plastic chairs. There was a clock hanging on the wall with a large white face and a sweeping red second hand. I watched it go all the way around once. It was 2:37. A table nearby held a few magazines that looked like about a million people had read them already. I pictured those million people licking their million spitty thumbs as they turned those same pages again and again, and I felt sick to my stomach.

My mother reached for a magazine with a picture of a big pie on the cover. I closed my eyes. When I opened them again, I looked up at the clock. It was 2:38.

"Can't somebody come out and tell us what's happening?" I asked.

"I'm sure as soon as anybody knows anything, they'll come and tell us, Guysie," my mom said, closing the magazine and putting it back on the table. "I know you're worried."

"*Worried?* No, that's too small a word to describe how I feel. You don't understand, Mom. You weren't there. You didn't see him. It was like he was Buzz, only he wasn't Buzz."

"I know, baby. I know." Her consoling didn't help—it just made me mad.

"No, you don't know!" I yelled, suddenly standing up and facing her. "Don't say you know, when you can't possibly know. Is he *your* best friend? Did *you* see him lying there not moving? Are you the one who . . ." I couldn't bring myself to say the horrible thing that ached and burned guiltily inside me. *Are you the one whose fault it is that Buzz got hurt?*

"I guess you're right, Guy. I can't know how you feel. But I love Buzzy too. You know that. He's like one of the family. I don't know what I'd do if anything happened to him." She pinched the bridge of her nose. She always does that when she's about to cry.

I felt bad that I'd yelled at her like that. It's true, my mom does love Buzz. She always has.

"I'm sorry," I said softly as I sat down next to her.

She put her arm around me, and I rested my head on her shoulder.

"What if he's not okay?" I asked.

"We can't think that way, Guysie," she said, sitting up straight and wiping her eyes and nose with a crumpled tissue she pulled out of her pocket. "No. We have to think positive. That's all there is to it."

"Positive, about what?" I asked.

"About Buzz," my mother answered. "Instead of imagining the worst, we have to visualize the best."

"What are you talking about?" I asked.

"Just the other day I was reading an article about how positive psychic energy has remarkable healing effects on the human body," she said. "It was fascinating."

"Mom, this isn't going to turn into a lecture about how blue food coloring and television commercials stunt your growth, is it?" I said warily.

"Of course not. I'm just saying that a lot of people believe that creating a positive aura around someone who's sick can help make them better."

"Okay, okay." I hate when my mother starts spouting about stuff like auras.

"We could try it," she said. "I mean, it can't hurt, right?"

I shrugged.

"They made it sound pretty easy. All you

have to do is think something positive about the person. For instance, right now I'm going to think about the look on Buzz's face when he bites into a warm snicker doodle. Can you picture that?" she asked.

Of course I could picture it. I'd seen him do it twelve million times. But I wasn't the least bit convinced it was going to do any good to sit there picturing Buzz eating cookies at a time like this.

"I can see him clear as day, with a huge smile on his face and a big cookie in each hand," my mother went on. "Now he's smiling at me and saying—"

"All reetie, baked ziti," I quietly finished the sentence for her. Buzz always says that when he's happy about something.

"Exactly!" my mother said. "See?"

"Not really," I said. "How do you know if it's working? Shouldn't something happen?"

"You have to put your faith in the idea that somehow your thoughts are going to reach Buzzy and make a difference. The positive cosmic energy will search high and low for him, and when it finds him, it'll wind around and around his spirit, and that will help begin to heal . . ."

I stopped listening. I know she meant well, but I have about zero tolerance for my mom's New-Agey junk. How do you wind a positive thought around someone, anyway? All I could picture was Buzz tangled up in a yo-yo string.

"At least give it a try, Guysie. It can't hurt. Besides, it's better than just sitting here worrying. Come on. Think about Buzz. Maybe some great time you had in the old fort. Or at camp. Or school. You guys have had a million terrific times together."

I closed my eyes and tried to picture Buzz. I sure had looked at his silly old freckled puss enough to have it memorized. But for some reason the first thing I pictured wasn't his face; it was his left sneaker. Why? And then I remembered. One of his shoes must have come off when the car hit him. I had seen it lying on its side in the gutter, with the laces still tied, a few feet away from where Buzz was lying on the pavement. As I pictured the empty shoe, I heard my own ridiculously happy voice coming back to me as I shouted to Buzz, "That's it, gum ball. Prepare to die!" The horrible relevance of those words made me sit up with a jolt.

"What's the matter?" my mother asked.

"I'm trying to think of positive stuff, but it's not working," I explained, still shaken by the image of that sneaker and the memory of those fateful words. *Prepare to die!* How could I have said that? I didn't mean it. I didn't mean it.

My mother put her arm around me, and I leaned against her again.

"Think back to the very beginning, Guy. When Buzzy first came to town. Do you remember that?" she said.

"Yeah, as a matter of fact we were kind of talking about that right before he—before the . . ."

I felt my chest tighten.

"Try not to think about the present, Honeybunch. Go back to the beginning. To the very first time you and Buzzy met each other. What a lucky thing that turned out to be, huh?"

I closed my eyes and let myself travel back in time. Memories spun in and out of focus, clicking into place like a slide show. My mom was right; meeting Buzz had turned out to be a lucky thing. The luckiest. But it hadn't exactly started out that way. . . .

Chapter Three

The summer before second grade started, I turned seven, and when I blew out the candles on my cake, I made the exact same wish I'd made the year before. And the year before that too. I wanted a best friend more than anything in the world.

Lana Zuckerman had Autumn Hockney. Max LeMott had Frankie Arches. Even Barry Madison, who was creepy and had a rotten front tooth, had a best friend. But I'd never had one. Not ever. I was pretty sure there was nothing wrong with me. People seemed to think I was a perfectly likeable, regular kind of kid, despite the fact that both of my parents were notoriously weird. So I figured that finding a best friend had more to do with luck—and that for some reason I was just unlucky.

My second-grade teacher was named Mrs. Hunn. She was pretty nice and hardly ever yelled at us unless we did something really bad like throwing wet paper-towel balls on the bathroom ceiling. She had neat stuff on her desk, which she didn't mind if we looked at as long as we didn't touch it. There was a framed picture of her water-skiing with her husband in Florida. A statue of the Empire State Building that had a ther-mometer in it that worked. And a little glass bell, which she rang whenever she had an announcement to make to the class.

I remember one day in the fall of that year—it must have been October, because I think we were making jack-o'-lanterns out of orange construction paper—Mrs. Hunn rang her bell, and when I looked up she was standing in front of her desk with her arm around this boy I'd never seen before. I knew right away that this was the new kid she'd been telling us was going to be joining our class. My heart sank. I'd been kind of hoping that my luck might change and he would turn out to be potential best-friend material. But that was obviously not going to be the case.

First of all, instead of jeans and a T-shirt, which is what all the rest of us boys had on, he was wearing a suit. A little blue jacket with matching pants, a bright white shirt, and a red-and-white-striped tie with a tiny tie pin shaped like a horseshoe stuck in it to hold it down flat against his shirtfront. His shoes were the lace-up kind, and they were two-toned—brown on the toes and heels and white on the sides. He had a white handkerchief sticking out of his jacket pocket. I repeat, a *handkerchief*. His pale face was splattered with a fistful of muddy freckles, and it was hard to tell what color his hair was because it was parted in the middle and flattened down on his head like a dark, wet helmet.

"Class, this is our new student, Fennimore Adams."

There was total silence. Then Kevin Brudhauser, the official class bully, spoke up. "What planet are you from?" he asked, grinning and looking around for approval as some of the other kids laughed.

"Fennimore comes to us all the way from Tennessee, Kevin," she said, giving Kev such an evil eye that it wiped the mean smile right off his face. "From a town called . . ." She hesitated as she tried to remember the name.

The boy piped up: "Pigeon Forge, Ma'am. It's south of Knoxville a piece."

When he spoke, a couple of the kids snickered, because he had a thick southern accent that made his words sound strange and twangy.

Mrs. Hunn went on to say the usual stuff about how she expected us all to give him a warm Cedar Springs welcome and show him the ropes until he was comfortable in his new surroundings. I just kept looking at that candy-cane-striped tie and those shoes and thinking, *It's a good thing geekiness isn't contagious, because this kid could be fatal.*

"Guy, I would like you to be Fennimore's lunch buddy today," Mrs. Hunn said.

Oh, man, I groaned to myself. *Why me?*

Then she turned to Fennimore and asked, "Did you bring lunch from home, dear, or will you be wanting hot lunch today?"

"My mama packed a lunch for me today, thank you kindly, Ma'am."

His *mama? Ma'am?* Why did I have to be his lunch buddy? Couldn't somebody else do it? It was bad enough that my mother packed me the weirdest lunches in the whole world. Now I had to eat my weird lunch with the weird new kid.

When the lunch bell rang, I shuffled slowly over to Fennimore's desk and waited while he put away his binder and spelling book.

"Come on," I said, when he was finally ready. I led him down the hall to the cafeteria, walking a little in front of him just so nobody would get the wrong idea and think we were friends.

"This cafeteria smells exactly the same as the one back in Pigeon Forge," he said when we walked through the doors.

"Uh-huh," I said without looking at him.

"Wanna hear my theory?" he asked.

I shrugged.

"I think there is this huge underground cave somewhere full of lady robots with hair nets and big moles on their chins. They program them to mix up giant vats of disgusting stuff like barbecued beef and pour it into big barrels. Then they load the barrels onto planes and drop them out of the sky like big beef bombs, *splat!* into cafeterias across the country."

I laughed. Even though it was hard to look at Fennimore in that ridiculous suit and feel anything other than pity for him, I had to admit, those barbecue beef bombs were pretty funny.

"I don't eat hot lunch," I said. "My mother packs mine."

"Mine too," he said with a smile, holding up his blue lunch box.

We sat down at a table near the door and put our lunch boxes out on the table in front of us. I watched as Fennimore opened his. He pulled out a peanut butter and jelly sandwich cut into two neat triangles, a box of apple juice, and a banana.

"I always used to trade with my best friend, George, back in Pigeon Forge," he said.

"Oh," I said. But I didn't open my box. I was thinking about two things. One, I was trying to imagine what George was like. Probably some polite little nerd in a dorky suit. And two, I was trying to avoid having to show Fennimore what was in my lunch box.

"Do you like to trade?" he asked, leaning over toward me and reaching for my lunch box. "Let's see whatcha got."

"No," I said, putting both hands on the box

and sliding it quickly over to the edge of the table, where I held it tightly against my chest.

"No problem," he said. "Some people don't like swapping. George always said my lunch was too boring to trade anyway. You probably got something way more interesting than PBJ, huh?"

"Maybe," I said, knowing full well that whatever my mother had packed was guaranteed to scoot right past "interesting" directly into the category of "totally bizarre."

Fennimore unwrapped his sandwich and bit off the soft point of one of the triangles. He smiled at me as he chewed, but I looked away. He seemed nice enough, and he had made me laugh with his lunch-lady robot theory, but there was no getting around the fact that Fennimore was a dork. The helmet hair alone was clear proof of that. And I wasn't about to befriend a dork. Life was hard enough as it was.

"Listen, " I said suddenly. "Now that you know where the cafeteria is and everything, you don't mind if I leave you here and go outside, do you? I sometimes like to play basketball during lunch with my friends when the weather's nice. So I'm gonna go now, okay?"

"Oh, sure. Okay," he said. He sounded a little disappointed, but how sorry could I feel for him? After all, he had a normal lunch in his lunch box and a best friend back home. He was pretty lucky. Me, I didn't even want to think about what ridiculous thing my mother had packed me for lunch, and it was depressing to think that even someone who had a silly name and walked around dressed up the way he was could have a best friend when I didn't have one.

"See you later," I said as I picked up my lunch box.

"Okay, " he said.

When I got outside, I found a bench far away from the basketball court and opened my lunch box. As soon as I saw the contents, I was glad I'd decided not to open it up in front of Fennimore. There was a tortilla stuffed with raisin bran cereal; three slices of American cheese, which she had cut out in the shapes of the letters GUY; and a can of guava juice. Occasionally my mother puts in something good for dessert, but this time she'd packed a long, hard skinny thing covered in brown sticky stuff, which was coated with tan crumbs. I had no idea what it was. As usual she'd written a note and taped it to the inside of the lid:

> Dear Guysie—hope you like my latest invention. I call it Rabbit Delight. Don't worry, it's not made of rabbit—it's a carrot covered with butterscotch sauce and peanuts. Enjoy!
> Love,
> Mom

I unrolled the tortilla and dumped out the raisin bran. Then I put the cheese inside it and rolled it back up and ate it. I tried the guava juice, but it was repulsive so I threw it and the Rabbit Delight in the trash. It wasn't exactly a satisfying meal, but believe it or not, I'd had worse. Sometimes the only normal thing in my lunch box was the napkin.

When I looked up, I saw that Fennimore was standing near the basketball court looking over toward me. I felt sort of bad, because I'd told him I was going out there to play ball, and he could probably tell that I'd just wanted to eat my lunch alone. He raised one hand and kind of half waved at me. I didn't wave back. I was not going to let my guilty conscience talk me into making the mistake of befriending this kid. My mother's public displays of wackiness already kept me plenty busy trying to maintain my image as just a normal, regular, seven-year-old boy. I couldn't afford to rock the boat.

I wanted a best friend more than anything in the world—but the one I'd been wishing for every time I blew out the birthday candles was definitely *not* Fennimore Adams.

Chapter Four

When we got back to the classroom after lunch, Mrs. Hunn rang her bell for the second time that same October day.

"Boys and girls, settle down. Settle down, please. As you know, our second-grade play, *The Princess and the Pea*, begins rehearsals this afternoon. Up until this morning we had absolutely no volunteers for the costume committee, but I'm very pleased to announce that we now have an enthusiastic chairperson who has volunteered to create original costumes for our entire production. Isn't that exciting news!"

"Who volunteered?" asked Frankie.

"Mrs. Strang. Guy's mother," said Mrs. Hunn.

"Oh, man," I said to myself. Could this day get any worse?

"As many of you know," Mrs. Hunn continued, "Guy's mother is a very, um, *creative* person, and I'm certain that her costumes will make a wonderful addition to our production."

"She's creative all right. Did anybody see what she did last Fourth of July?" Kevin said loudly. "She's nuts!"

I wasn't about to disagree with him. What she'd done was wrap red, white, and blue crepe paper all the way around our station wagon *and* herself and drive through town honking her horn and waving sparklers out the window. To make matters worse, she had convinced my father to dress up as the Statue of Liberty. He stood up on the passenger seat with his head sticking out of the sunroof, wearing an old green bathrobe and a cut-up wastebasket crown on his head.

"That's nothing. What about what she wore to the first-grade class picnic!" said Lana Zuckerman, the tallest, meanest girl in the class. "Remember that?"

Actually she was the tallest kid, boy *or* girl, in the whole grade, and she would have been the meanest too, except that Kevin had that position filled. If you'd told me then that a few years later my parents would get divorced and my mother would get re-married to *Lana Zuckerman's father,* I would have found the nearest cliff and thrown myself off it. But anyway, Lana was on a roll, reminding everybody about that embarrassing class picnic the year before.

"We all saw your bare buttonhole, Guy!" She laughed, and so did everybody else who knew what she was talking about.

At the picnic my mother had showed up wearing a vest she'd made by taking a bunch of my baby photos, punching holes in the corners, and sewing them together with yarn. I don't mean just any baby photos. I'm talking photographs of me sitting on the potty, having my diaper changed, and rolling around in the backyard wearing nothing but a Big Bird bib. My bare *buttonhole*, as Lana called it, had been on display for everyone to see.

"Class, that's enough now. As I said, we are all most fortunate to have Mrs. Strang on board for our production."

When I got home that afternoon, my mother was in the kitchen frosting a cake.

"Hi, honeybunch," she called as I came in the back door and dropped my book bag in the corner.

"Why didn't you ask me if I wanted you to make costumes for the play?" I asked.

"Well, why wouldn't you want me to?" she said, pausing for a second with a rubber spatula full of chocolate frosting in her hand. "You can't do a play without costumes, and Mrs. Hunn practically kissed my feet when I volunteered."

I looked down at my mother's feet. Her

toenails, each one painted a different color, were sticking out of the fronts of her tropical-fruit sandals—just one of her many exotic creations. She'd taken a pair of regular white shoes and hot-glue-gunned plastic fruit—strawberries, grapes, and pineapple chunks—all over them. I tried to imagine Mrs. Hunn kissing them.

"This production of *The Princess and the Pea* is going to be unlike any production ever done before," she announced proudly.

"I believe that," I said. "Let me guess, are you planning to hot-glue fruit all over every-body?"

"I don't know about fruit," she said. "But maybe some little green peas would be cute!"

"I was kidding, Mom," I said.

My mother smiled at me and handed me one of the beaters. I ran my tongue along the chocolatey edge. Then I gagged and hurried to the sink to spit out what I had thought was frosting but what I knew the second it collided with my tastebuds was definitely *not*.

"What *is* that?" I said as soon as I was able to speak.

"Chocolate pâté," she said.

"What's pâté?" I asked as I grabbed a glass, filled it with water, and swished out my mouth.

"Liver," she said.

"Liver?" I said, "You're making a *liver* cake?"

"It's not supposed to be a dessert; it's more of an appetizer. I made it up," she said.

"Yeah, I can tell." I tried to wipe the last of the sickening flavor off my tongue with a wet paper towel. "Next time warn me, will you?"

"I'm sorry, Guysie. How about a cookie?"

"What's in them—brussels sprouts?" I asked.

"No surprises. I promise," she said as I opened the cookie jar and pulled out a cookie.

"Milk?" she asked.

I nodded, and she poured me a glass of

cold milk. We heard a car door slam. My father was home.

"Wuckums!" my mother called as she ran to the door to greet him.

My father's real name is William, but he couldn't say it when he was a kid so he called himself Wuckums instead. It probably stuck because it actually fit him much better than William.

"What's that wonderful smell?" he asked, whiffing the air in the kitchen. "Kind of choco-latey yet at the same time—do I detect a hint of liver?"

"It's chocolate pâté. I invented it myself," my mother said proudly.

"How exotic! Just like you, my little dump truck," my father said, kissing my mother's cheek with a loud smack.

I often wondered what it would be like to have a father who called his wife "darling" instead of "dump truck," not to mention a mother who knew that liver and chocolate don't go together.

"How was your day at school, Guychik?" my father asked.

"Tell him the big news!" my mother said excitedly.

"What big news?" I asked.

"About the play, silly," she prompted.

"My class is putting on a play," I said flatly. It hardly seemed like big news to me.

"It's *The Princess and the Pea*, and I'm doing the costumes!" my mother declared.

"Fantastic!" my father said enthusiastically. "What part are you playing, Guy?"

"I'm a shrub," I said.

"A *shrub*?" my mother asked, wrinkling up her brow, "I don't remember any shrubbery in the version of the story I read. Do you, Wuck?"

"I don't think I've ever read it," my father replied. "I'm strictly a sci-fi guy."

"The shrubs were Mrs. Hunn's idea. Since there aren't enough real parts to go around, some of us are playing bushes that grow around the castle walls," I explained.

"Did you try out for one of the real parts, Guysie? Wouldn't you rather be a person than a bush?" my mother asked.

"Nah, I don't like drama. The shrubs don't have to do anything except sit there looking bushy, and that sounds just right to me."

"Who else is playing a shrub?" Dad asked.

"A bunch of us. All boys. Max, Greg, Alex, and Henry. Oh, and Fennimore."

"Fennimore?" my mother said.

"Yeah, he's the new kid."

"Fennimore is a very unusual name. What's he like?" she asked.

"Like his name," I replied. "*Unusual.*"

"Maybe he'll turn out to be your new best friend," said my mother with a big smile.

"Nope," I said. "That's not going to happen."

"How can you say that? You've barely even met him," my father said. "The most interesting people often turn out to be the ones who take a little longer to get to know, don't you think, dumpers?"

"Abso-tootin-lutely," my mother agreed.

"Trust me, Fennimore and I are not going to be best friends. For one thing, I don't want an unusual friend," I said, picking up my book bag and heading upstairs to start my homework. "When I find a best friend, I want him to be regular. Like me."

I thought about Fennimore later that night as I lay in bed trying to go to sleep. Why couldn't the new kid have been someone with a normal name, like Alex or David or Sam? And a regular haircut and clothes. Why couldn't he have been someone I could talk to about stuff? Share secrets with. Invite for sleepovers and all the other things best friends do together. Why couldn't he have been just right instead of, well . . . Fennimore.

Chapter Five

The rehearsals were for our second-grade production of *The Princess and the Pea* were pretty boring, especially for those of us who were playing shrubs. Lana and Kevin were the king and queen, so they had a lot of lines to rehearse. Nico DePalma, who everybody thought was so cute on account of his dimples and wavy black hair, was playing the prince. Then there were the princesses, who were played by the girlie-girls in the class—Autumn, Kendra, Sawyer, and Grace. They had speeches to practice too. All the other characters had a few lines here and there, but the shrubs didn't say anything at all. Mrs. Hunn suggested that we might want to make up a little bush dance to do to make our parts more interesting, but we took a vote, and it was unanimously decided that we would be a nondancing variety of shrubbery.

"Suit yourselves," she said, and went back to the read-through of the script.

I spent most of the second rehearsal staring at Bob-o Smith, who was playing a castle guard. He was supposed to say "Halt, who goes there?" whenever anyone approached the castle, but he wasn't following along in his script, so he missed his cues every time. Each time he messed up, Lana would kick him under the table, and Bob-o would jump and say, "What did I do?" in a high squeaky voice. Lana quickly lost patience with him.

"If I were really the queen and you were my guard, I'd fire you so fast, your head would spin," she grumped.

"Forget about making it spin. Why don't we save time and just behead him instead?" suggested King Kevin.

"Great idea, your majesty," said Lana.

"Who needs a guard anyway? We could just booby-trap the castle gate to keep out the undesirables."

"Far out. Strap some dynamite to it, and whoever shows up—*kaboom!*" Kevin said, making explosive spitty noises with his big, ugly, wet mouth.

"All I can say is it's a good thing you two aren't really the king and queen around here," said Mrs. Hunn with a sigh. "I have a feeling more than one of us would be walking around without a head on our shoulders."

Bob-o didn't seem to be aware that he had been insulted. He was completely oblivious, as usual. He'd been in my class every year since kindergarten, and he seemed to get stranger and stranger with each passing year. While I watched him that day, I remember, he was doing something bizarre. He'd pull on one of his eyebrows really hard, and whenever he managed to pull out a hair, he'd put it in the palm of his hand, close his eyes, and blow on it. Then he'd study his hand really carefully to see if the hair was still there, and if it was, he'd do it all over again.

"Making wishes," whispered Fennimore, who was sitting behind me.

"Huh?" I said, not sure what he was talking about. "Who's making wishes?"

"That goofy kid in the glasses. Bob-o. He's making wishes on his eyebrows," he said.

"Really?" I watched Bob-o, who had just pulled out another hair. He placed it in his palm and closed his eyes. His lips moved a little like he was saying something to himself, then he blew on the hair and checked to see if it was gone.

"See, if the hair is gone after he blows on it, the wish comes true," Fennimore explained.

Just then, right while we were both looking at him, Bob-o stuck his finger way up his nose and started digging for gold, as they say.

"Sheesh," said Fennimore, flinching at the sight of it. "I guess maybe he was wishing for a tissue and it didn't come true."

I laughed out loud, and Mrs. Hunn shot me a look over the tops of her glasses. Fennimore immediately stood up.

"Excuse us for being rude, Ma'am; we didn't mean to bother you. It won't happen again."

Mrs. Hunn looked kind of surprised. I'd never seen anybody do what Fennimore had just done, and I guess she hadn't either. He fessed up and apologized without even trying to deny it first. Mrs. Hunn smiled and nodded and went back to work.

"Wow. Are you always that polite?" I whispered.

"Who, me? Listen to this." He tucked his chin down and swallowed air; then he let loose a long, rumbling belch. As he burped, he moved his lips to form words—the letters of the alphabet. He ran out of steam, or rather belch, around the letter "p." It was amazing and gross and funny. All in all, pretty great.

"Rude!" I said appreciatively.

"Jumbo rude," he said back.

This time I was careful to cover my laughter with a fake coughing fit. Mrs. Hunn looked up again, but she didn't say anything.

"Maybe we should try wishing on our eyebrows that this stupid rehearsal would end already," I said when I'd recovered enough to speak.

He smiled and nodded, and we both tugged on our eyebrows at the same time. Then we closed our eyes and blew on the hairs. When I opened my eyes, the hair was gone, and right then the final bell rang. I looked over at Fennimore, and he grinned at me.

"Guess it works, huh, Gah Wahr?" he said.

"Gah Wahr?" I said, repeating what it sounded like he'd said.

"Yeah, Gah," he said, pointing to me. "Wahr."

"Oh, you mean, *Guy*." I finally understood.

"But what does Wahr mean?"

"Wahr, like on a telephone pole," he said.

"Oh, you mean *wire?*"

He nodded.

"Guy Wire?" I said.

"Yeah, *Guy Wire,*" he said, stretching his mouth around the words in order to change his accent and make it sound more the way it did when I said it.

"What's a guy wire?" I asked.

"It's like a support wire that goes out kind of sideways on radio towers to keep them from falling over. You know?"

"Uh, no," I said.

"Sure you do, they go out sideways, sort of at an angle like this." He held up his hands to try to demonstrate, but it didn't help. I had absolutely no idea what he was talking about. And why was he calling me that—was he trying to say I was skinny like a wire or something? That was kind of insulting, especially coming from someone who had helmet hair like his.

"I don't get it," I said.

"There's nothing to get, really. It's not supposed to mean anything. I just thought it might make sort of a cool nickname because, well you know, because it has *Guy* already built into it and all," he said as he hoisted his book bag onto one shoulder.

"Oh," I said.

"If you don't like it, though, I won't call you that. I'll come up with something else, if you want," he said. "See ya."

"Yeah. See ya, Fennimore," I said as I watched him leave.

I stood there for a minute thinking. I was pretty surprised. I mean, my mother calls me Guysie and my father calls me Guychik, but nobody outside the family had ever given me a nickname before. Why would Fennimore want to give me a nickname?

Guy Wire. Huh. Now that I thought about it, it did have kind of a nice ring to it.

Chapter Six

On the way home I noticed Fennimore walking up ahead of me. He was wearing jeans and sneakers and a blue down jacket. Without his suit on he looked pretty much like everybody else. Except for one thing. His hair was still hopelessly nerdy.

"Hey, Fennimore," I called. "Wait up."

Fennimore turned around, and when he recognized me, he smiled and waved and waited for me to catch up.

"You live around here?" he asked when I reached him.

"Yeah, on Maple; what about you?"

"I live on Robin," he said.

"Oh, that's just a couple of blocks past my house," I said.

"You ever notice how they always name streets after things like birds and trees?" he asked.

"Yeah," I said. "So what?"

"So it's too bad they pick such boring ones," he said.

"What do you mean?" I asked.

"Wouldn't you rather live on Venus's-Flytrap Street than boring old Maple?" he asked.

"I guess," I said, "But a Venus's-Flytrap is a plant, not a tree."

"Okay, but if it's a bird street, wouldn't it be cooler if it was, like, Blue-Footed Boobie Boulevard?" he said.

"Sure, if there was such a bird as a blue-footed boobie," I said.

"There is," he said.

"No way," I said.

"Way. I've got a book with a picture of one in it at my house. I can show you if you want."

We were at the corner of my street.

"This is my block," I said, pointing down the street toward my house.

"I know, but don't you want to see the boobie?" he asked.

"Now?" I said.

"Sure," he said.

"Well, okay, I guess, but I gotta ask my mom," I said. I hesitated for a minute. "Do you wanna come with me?"

"Sure."

Fennimore and I headed down the street to my house. I stopped when we got to the front walk.

"Listen, I have to warn you about something," I said as we started up my driveway. "The name of my street may be boring and ordinary, but my parents are a whole different story."

"Is it true your mama showed everybody bare naked pictures of you at the class picnic last year?"

I nodded.

"Sheesh," he said. "Is she touched?"

"Touched?"

"Yeah, you know, touched in the head," Fennimore said, tapping his temple with his finger.

"Oh, you mean crazy?"

He nodded.

As if to answer his question, right as we were walking up the porch steps, the back door burst open, and my mother came running out of the house wearing a bathing cap covered with green cotton balls and a piece of Astroturf with pom-pom fringe tied around her shoulders.

"What do you think?" she shouted as she ran past us down the steps and zoomed around the backyard waving her arms like a maniac. "I'm a shrub!"

"Holy crow!" said Fennimore, taking it all in with wide eyes.

"I told you," I said, watching my mother round the far corner of the yard, bank like an airplane, and head back our way.

"Who's your little friend, Guysie?" she said, stopping to catch her breath and joining us on the porch.

"Mom, this is Fennimore. Fennimore . . . meet my mom."

Fennimore politely stuck his hand out.

"How do you do, Ma'am," he said. "That's a very nice, uh, bathing cap you've got on there."

My mother shook his hand and laughed delightedly.

"Well, aren't you just as cute as a button."

Fennimore blushed.

"Being as cute as you are, though, do you mind my asking what in the world possessed you to wear your hair that way?" my mother asked.

"*Mom,*" I said rolling my eyes. She's always blurting things out like that. She calls it "being frank." As far as I'm concerned, whoever this Frank guy is, he's very rude.

"No, it's okay," Fennimore reassured me. "Is something wrong with my hair, Mrs. Strang?"

"Nothing that a little trim couldn't fix," my mother said. "Come on inside, and I can fix you up in a jiff."

"I don't think my mama would want me to get a haircut without her here," Fennimore said quietly.

"You call your mother *mama*? Oh, I just love that! It's so, so *regional*. Tell you what," my mother said. "Why don't you call your mama up and ask her if it's all right for you to get a little trim. Tell her she's welcome to come watch me work my magic if she'd like to. I can trim hers too, for that matter, if she wants. We'll make a party of it."

Fennimore looked at me. I shrugged.

"She cuts mine," I said. "And no offense, but to be honest, your hair is a little, well, *flat*."

Fennimore touched his head.

"That's on account of all the cowlicks," he explained. "If I don't plaster it down, it looks like crabgrass."

"I assure you, with a proper trim those

cowlicks would lie down flat without one drop of hair goop," my mother said. "Trust me."

She opened the door and held it for us.

"I've been cutting Guy's hair ever since he was a little boy," my mom told Fennimore. "And I cut his father's hair too. If I say so myself, I'm pretty darned good at it. Do you want a cookie?"

My mother handed Fennimore a cookie out of the cookie jar. He bit into it and moaned.

"What's the matter? Sore tooth?" she asked.

"Uh-uh." Fennimore shook his head. "*Sweet* tooth. My mom gives me rice cakes after school on account of all the fillings I've had to get. Do they have rice cakes in Cedar Springs?"

"Of course," she said.

"I was afraid of that." Fennimore took another bite of cookie.

"Okay, Guy, show Fennimore where the phone in the den is so he can call his mama in private. I'll find my scissors, and if she gives us the go-ahead, we can get started." She held up her hands and made a little frame out of her index fingers and thumbs and squinted at Fennimore through it like an artist looks at a bowl of fruit before she paints it. "I love a challenge," she said.

Fennimore called home and spoke to his mother. After he hung up, he came back into the kitchen, where my mom and I were waiting.

"Is she going to join us?" my mother asked him.

"No, Mrs. Strang. She's making a stew, but she says to thank you kindly for the offer and that it's okay for you to cut my hair so long as it's just a little trim."

"Good! A little trim it is then," my mother said, going and pulling some towels out of the hall closet. "Guy, drag that stool over, will you?"

I pulled the stepstool out into the center of the room.

"Before we get started, do you think I might trouble you for another one of those delicious cookies, Mrs. Strang?" Fennimore asked politely.

"Oh, those manners! Good gravy, have as many cookies as you want, you angel boy!" she said, handing him the whole jar.

It was true that my mother had cut my hair for years, and she'd never done anything weird to it, so I was pretty sure that whatever she had in mind for Fennimore would be fine. Besides, his hair was already weird, so she couldn't possibly make it any worse.

"Okay, Fennimore," she said cheerfully. "First of all we'll need to wash your hair."

My mother took Fennimore over to the kitchen sink and made him bend over with his head under the faucet. It took three washings to get out whatever he'd put in there to hold it down flat. Then she wrapped the towel around his head.

"Lawrence of Suburbia!" She laughed.

Fennimore sat on the kitchen stool happily

munching cookies while my mother wrapped a beach towel around his shoulders and began to comb his hair.

"How long do you think this is gonna take?" he asked.

"A little trim takes two shakes of a lamb's tail," she answered.

"Mom, speak English, will you? It's three thirty right now, and all he wants to know is—oh my gosh, oh my gosh!"

"What's the matter?" my mother asked.

"I've got soccer practice. Right now! I completely forgot. I was supposed to be there at three thirty. My coach is gonna kill me. Quick, Mom, where's my uniform?"

I started running around trying to pull my jeans off over my sneakers without sitting down. My shoes got jammed in the legs of the pants, and I tripped and fell down on the floor.

"Relax, Guysie. Nobody's going to kill you. I'll write you a note."

"A *note*? What are you, *nuts*?" I said, finally

managing to yank my pants off. "Mothers don't write notes to soccer coaches. Please, just tell me where my uniform is."

"I washed it last night. It's probably still in the dryer."

I stopped dead in my tracks.

"You put it in the dryer?"

"Yes."

"Remember I told you not to do that because it might shrink and it was already too small to begin with?"

"Oh, I'm sorry. You did tell me that, didn't you, sweetie?"

I ran down into the basement in my underwear and yanked open the dryer. Crossing my fingers, I reached into the warm, dark drum.

"How is it?" my mother called from upstairs.

How it was, was *horrible*. The shorts were so tight I could barely get them on, the shirt had shrunk to the point that you could see my bellybutton if I lifted my arms, and the socks didn't even reach my knees anymore. There was nothing I could do about it; I was already late for practice. I ran back up the stairs and into the kitchen.

"Oh, dear," my mother said when she saw me. "That does look a little snug. Do you want me to try to let out a seam or two?" She stepped toward me with the scissors.

"Don't come any closer," I said, holding up my hands. "You've done enough already."

Fennimore was still sitting on the stool with the towel around his shoulders. He looked a little overwhelmed.

"I'm sorry," I said to him. "I completely forgot about my practice. We can go to your house and look up the blue-footed boobie tomorrow if you want."

"Okay," he said. He started to take off the towel. "Maybe we'd better do the trim another day too, Mrs. Strang."

"Nonsense," she said. "We'll be finished before you know it."

"I've gotta go," I said, rushing toward the door. "'Bye, Fennimore! Sorry!"

The last thing I saw before I slammed the door shut behind me was my mother with her long silver scissors poised over Fennimore's head.

Chapter Seven

An hour and a half later I came home, tired and sweaty. My soccer shorts had completely split up the back the first time I'd kicked the ball, and the shirt had torn open under both arms right after that. The coach scrounged around and dug up the only extra uniform. It was a size husky, and because everyone on my team was pretty scrawny like me, nobody had been able to use it. It's a good thing you don't need your hands for soccer, because mine were both busy the whole time trying to keep my clothes on. I was exhausted.

As I headed up the walk to my house, yanking up my shorts for about the twelve millionth time, I was surprised to see Fennimore sitting on the back porch with his head in his hands. He was wearing his jacket and a knit hat I thought I recognized as one of my father's pulled way down over his ears.

"Fennimore?" I said. "What are you doing out here?"

He raised his head. He looked like he'd been crying.

"What's the matter?" I said.

Speechlessly he reached up and slowly removed his hat.

"Oh, man," I whispered when I saw what the matter was. "Man oh man oh man."

He wasn't exactly bald, but my mother had managed to get him about as close to it as you can get without actually being there. His whole head was fuzzy like a peach.

"Wow. You look—you look *different*," I said. I knew it was a dumb thing to say, but it was the best I could come up with.

"Just a little trim? Yeah, right, she distracted

me with cookies and then she sheared me like a sheep." A fat tear slid down his cheek and he brushed it away with the back of his hand. "My mama is gonna *kill* me."

"It'll grow back," I said.

"Unless it grows back by the time I get home, I'm gonna get switched."

"It's not your fault, Fennimore. My mother said she was only gonna give you a little trim. I heard her. I'll make sure she tells your mom that. Promise."

Fennimore reached into his pocket and pulled out a folded slip of blue paper. I recognized the stationery. My mother's.

"She wrote me a note," he said.

I took it from him and read it.

Dear Mrs. Adams:

I'm afraid I got a little carried away trimming Fennimore's hair this afternoon. He's quite concerned about your reaction, but I've assured him that although it wasn't my original intention to give him

a buzz cut, the look actually suits him
quite well. I hope you'll agree.

Sincerely,

Lorraine Strang

P.S. Fennimore asked to borrow a hat.
No hurry to return it; my husband has
others should the weather turn cold.

P.P.S. Would you and your family care to
join us for fondue some night next week?

I folded it and handed it back to Buzz.

"Do you want me to go yell at her?"
I asked.

"What good is that going to do?"
Fennimore stood up and brushed off the
seat of his pants. "It is what it is."

"I shouldn't have left you here alone with
her," I said. "I'm sorry. She's always been okay
with my hair. Honest. I had no idea she could
do something like—like *that*." I pointed at his
fuzzy head.

Fennimore put the hat back on and pulled it low over his ears. "You know, before we moved, everybody told me I was gonna love it here. People in the Midwest are so *friendly*, they kept saying. Well, so far all anybody around here's been doing is making fun of the way I talk and dress and telling me I need to fix my hair different. I was just fine where I came from. I wish I'd never left."

He was raising his voice. I felt awful.

"Do you know what they call me behind my back at school?" he asked me, his voice getting louder still.

I knew, but I didn't want to say.

"Southern Fried Chicken Boy." Another tear spilled down his face. "Can you imagine what they're gonna be calling me when they get a load of this haircut?"

"I'll tell everybody what happened," I said. "Maybe my mom can come talk to the class or something."

"Like that's gonna help. Everybody already knows your mother's nuts. They'll say it was my own fault. They'll say I was crazy to come over here with you, knowing what kind of family you come from."

My throat burned from trying to hold back my own tears now.

"I'm not really like them," I said quietly.

Fennimore snorted.

"Where I come from we have an expression for people like you. 'The apple doesn't fall far from the tree,'" he said. Then he started down the sidewalk.

"Do you want me to come home with you? To help explain things to your mom?" I called after him.

"Don't bother," he said without looking at me.

I watched him turn up the block, his hat pulled down low, his head hanging, and his hands shoved angrily into his pockets. His whole body spelled misery.

"I'll see you in school tomorrow, Fennimore!" I shouted.

But he didn't even turn around.

Chapter Eight

"**H**ow could you do this to me!" I yelled as I banged in the door and stomped into the kitchen, where my mother was fixing a salad for dinner.

"I'm sorry, sugar pleat. I told you I forgot I wasn't supposed to put your uniform in the dryer. Come over here, and let me look at those pants you've got on. Criminy, they're huge, but don't worry, a couple of quick tucks will make them snug."

"I'm not talking about my uniform, Mom. I'm talking about what you did to Fennimore."

"You mean his hair?" she asked.

"What hair? He's *bald*, Mom."

"He's not bald, for heaven's sake, but it is shorter than I'd intended it to be. I started off trimming it just the way I do yours, Guysie, but I had trouble getting it even. Those cowlicks of his are murder. I kept having to take off a little more here and then a little bit more there trying to even it up. So I tried doing it with your father's electric beard clipper, and pretty soon, somehow or other—"

"You accidentally cut off all his hair and ruined his life," I finished the sentence for her.

"Oh, pooh," she said, giving the salad a last whirl in the spinner. "A person's life can't be ruined by a little haircut. It's just going to take some getting used to is all. If you want my honest opinion, I think now he really looks cute as a button."

"Are you for real?" I asked. "You think he looks *cute*?"

"All the boys I knew back in high school wore their hair like that. It's a classic buzz cut. And it certainly suits him better than that plastered-down look," she said, taking the top off the spinner and popping a piece of lettuce into her mouth.

"Mom!" I shouted. "You wrecked Fennimore's hair. Don't try to convince yourself that you didn't. And that's not all you wrecked either. You wrecked my chance of being friends with him too."

"Nonsense," my mother said. "He told me you're the only one at school who's really made an effort to be nice to him. He's dying to be your friend, Guysie."

"That was before you scalped him, Mom. He's not even speaking to me anymore."

My mother was quiet.

"I know he was upset," she said after a minute. "He wouldn't leave here until I found him a hat to put on. But it will grow back. Hey, you know what I'm going to do? I'm going to make him a batch of cookies and take them over to his house right now. That boy eats snicker doodles like there's no tomorrow."

"You're not going over to his house. You're not going near him ever again. If you didn't insist on acting weird in front of every single person I know, maybe I'd have found a best friend by now. Did it ever occur to you that maybe it's your fault that I haven't?"

"I didn't mean to cut his hair so short," she said. "I wrote his mother a note. I even asked them to dinner next week. Let's see what she says. I'm sure Fennimore will come around, sugar pleat."

"Oh, I get it, you shave Fennimore's head, ruin our friendship before it's even started, and then expect it all to miraculously disappear because you're inviting his family to one of your bizarre-o dinner parties? What the heck is fondue, anyway? And why are you calling me sugar pleat?"

"Fondue is a festive interactive cheese dish, and sugar pleat is a combination of sugar plum and sweet pea. It's a term of endearment, you know, a nickname, like—"

I clapped my hands over my ears.

"I don't want to hear this, Mom. I don't want to hear about interactive cheese and I don't want a nickname—not from *you*, anyway."

"What's that supposed to mean?" she asked.

"You wouldn't understand," I muttered.

The phone rang, and she went to answer it.

"Oh, Mrs. Adams"—my mom shot me a quick look—"how do you do. I'm so glad you called. If it's about the haircut, I can explain . . . uh-huh . . . Yes, yes it *is* quite short, but it was an honest mistake. You see, I was trying to even it out and . . . What did you say? . . . Really? . . . *You do?* You *like* it? . . . Well, isn't that wonderful!" My mother shot me another look, this one triumphant and a little smug. "Call me Lorraine, why don't you. . . . Okay then, Barbara it is. . . . What's that? Oh, you *would*? I'm so glad. In fact, I'm abso-tootin-lutely tickled!"

She put her hand over the receiver and

whispered to me: "She says they'd love to come to dinner next week. And she *loves* Fennimore's haircut. Seems Fennimore's father had one just like it back in the old days. So there, smarty pants." Then she went back to her conversation with Fennimore's mother.

"How about Sunday night? . . . That's good? . . . Great. We'll see you then. Right-o. Bye-bye!"

My mother smiled and shrugged her shoulders.

"You see, I told you it would all work out in the end, Guysie. Fennimore's mother said she's been trying to convince him to cut his hair shorter for years. They're all coming to dinner on Sunday."

I was shocked at the way this was turning out, but mostly I was relieved. Maybe Fennimore wouldn't stay mad at me. He might even be over it by the morning. He might even be over it already. After all, his mom wasn't mad. I thought about calling him up right then and there to find out where I stood, but I decided not to press my luck. He might need a little more time to get used to his new look.

I went to bed that night feeling pretty hopeful that Fennimore would forgive me. He was going to have to deal with whatever mean stuff kids at school said about his hair, but I'd help him do that. Together we would get through it. Together. I liked the sound of that. Maybe, just maybe, Fennimore had potential after all.

I thought about the conversation we'd had about the names of the streets in the neighborhood. That was pretty funny. Blue-Footed Boobie Boulevard. I laughed right out loud remembering that. And I thought about the way he'd belched the alphabet too. How cool was that? I smiled as I remembered something else. Fennimore Adams wanted to give me a nickname. Guy Wire. I decided to tell him the next day that I liked that name just fine.

Chapter Nine

I heard Kevin Brudhauser's obnoxious booming voice as I entered the school yard the next morning.

"Hey, look, everybody. The Southern Fried Chicken's been plucked!" he shouted.

I knew this meant that Fennimore had arrived ahead of me. I hurried to find him and help him out. He was sitting on a bench by the basketball courts.

"Hey," I said. "How you doing?"

"*Bruck, bruck, bruck*, the bird's been plucked!" Kevin taunted Fennimore from the other side of the court.

"How am I doing?" Fennimore asked bitterly. "Oh, just swell."

Then he got up and walked away. So much for thinking things were going to be okay between us. He was just as mad today as he had been the day before.

All day Fennimore avoided me. I tried sitting with him at lunch, but he got up and moved as soon as I sat down. I wrote him a note and passed it to him during science, but he tossed it in the trash without even reading it. Kevin taunted and teased him all day, and I'm not sure who felt worse about it, Fennimore or me.

That afternoon, when I got home, my mother asked about how it had gone.

"He hates me more than ever, thanks to you."

"I don't see what the problem is. Mrs. Adams told me she loves the haircut, so he certainly didn't get in trouble at home."

"Mom, it doesn't matter what his mother thinks. Don't you get it? Kids made fun of him all day."

"Well, I think he looks—"

"If you say 'cute as a button' one more time, I'm going to start screaming."

I took my backpack upstairs and spent the next hour doing homework. At four o'clock I couldn't concentrate anymore. I decided to go over to Fennimore's. I knew he lived on Robin Street, so I rode my bike the two blocks over and started looking for his house. Finally I spotted him sitting on his front stoop, bouncing a tennis ball on the steps. When he caught sight of me, he got up and started to go inside.

"Wait!" I cried, jumping off my bike and running across his yard. "I'm sorry, Fennimore, I'm really sorry about your hair. You've got to believe me when I say I had no idea my mother was going to botch it so badly. Let me make it up to you."

He stopped with his hand on the door-knob.

"How are you going to do that?"

"Well, I sort of thought of a plan."

"I'm listening," he said.

"You could pretend to be sick and stay home until it grows back," I suggested. "I could bring you the homework so you wouldn't get behind."

"That's lame," he said. "Everybody's already seen my hair. Don't you think they'd figure out why I wasn't coming to school?"

"I guess so," I said. "But there has to be something we can do."

"We don't have to do anything," he said.

He went inside, slamming the door behind him.

I rode home and went straight to my room. I pulled out a sheet of paper and a pencil and began to think hard. There had to be something I could do to fix things up with Fennimore. I came up with a few possibilities.

The first idea I had was to sneak into Kevin Brudhauser's house at night and shave his head. The plan was appealing, but there were some obvious problems with it. One, I wasn't allowed to go out alone after dark.

Two, Kevin lives on the other side of town, so my mother would have to drive me and wait while I cut off his hair.

I moved on to Plan B. Pretend to be the principal. Call up Mrs. Brudhauser and tell her Kevin was being suspended for a month. That would give Fennimore's hair time to grow back. I liked this plan a lot better. I pulled out the Cedar Springs phone book and looked up Brudhauser. Before dialing the number, I practiced speaking like Principal Cappert. He has kind of a high whining voice, and after a few tries I thought I was coming pretty close to it.

I dialed the number and let it ring three times. Kevin picked it up.

"Hello, young man, may I speak to your mother, please?" I said in my best Cappert imitation yet.

"Strang, is that you?" he said.

I hung up immediately. So much for Plan B.

And then it hit me. How could I have missed it? There was one and only one way to make it up to Fennimore. It was pretty extreme, but I was willing to do it.

"Mom!" I called as I ran down the stairs. "Get the clippers!"

Chapter Ten

"**A**re you sure about this, Guysie?" my mother asked.

"Positive."

"I'm not sure it's really you," she said reluctantly.

"I don't care," I said. "I'm not doing it for me, I'm doing it for Fennimore. I don't want him to have to bear it alone."

"That's awfully nice of you, honeybunch. You must really care about him, huh?"

When I'd first laid eyes on him, I'd been completely convinced that he and I would never be friends, but now I was ready to cut off all my hair just to make him feel better. I guess she was right. I did care about Fennimore.

"Go ahead," I said to my mother. "Do your worst."

She pinned a towel around my neck and went to work on me.

A half hour later I reached up and ran my hand over my head. It felt like muskrat fur. Not that I've ever petted an actual muskrat.

"What do you think?" I asked my mother.

"Well, to be frank, it's going to take some getting used to," she said.

I think I would have preferred to hear something more along the lines of "You look as cute as a button too," but when I looked at myself in the mirror, I had to agree with her. It was going to take some getting used to.

That night, as I went to sleep, I tried to imagine the look on Fennimore's face when he saw what I had done for him.

The next day was Saturday. As soon as I was up and dressed, I hopped on my bike and went over to Fennimore's house. I couldn't wait to show him my hair. As I rode up his driveway, I heard a basketball bouncing behind the garage. Figuring it was Fennimore, I headed around the back. The boy bouncing the ball wasn't Fennimore at all. He was tall, with a full head of dark curly hair and a sharp look to his face that immediately put me on edge.

"Who are you?" I asked.

"Who are *you?*" he shot back.

"I'm Fennimore's friend Guy," I said.

"Well, I'm his *best* friend, George," he said. He had the same kind of twangy accent as Fennimore.

"Where's Fennimore?" I asked.

"Inside finishing breakfast. I flew up here yesterday to surprise him. Boy, was he glad to see me."

Fennimore came out.

"Hey, what are you doing here?" he asked me. "Sheesh, what the heck happened to *your* hair?"

"Looks like he got scalped, same as you,

Fenn," George cackled, and he spat in the grass.

"Really, Guy, what's with your hair?" Fennimore said again. "You look worse than I do. Why did you let her do that?"

"I thought, I just thought, well, maybe it would help—"

"The only thing that's gonna help you now is a bag over your head." George cackled and spat again. "Hey, wait a minute. Is this the kid whose mama skinned you, Fenn? The same one you told me ran around showing his bare butt at a class picnic or something?"

"I did not!" I shouted.

"That's how I heard it," said George. "Come on, Fennimore, let's get out of here. This kid is giving me the creeps. Besides, his mama might be right behind him with her shears, and I don't want to lose my hair too."

"Guy, you really shouldn't have done it," Fennimore said.

"Yeah. No kidding," added George.

"I did it for you, Fennimore," I said. "To show we're friends."

"Some friend," George sneered.

"You really shouldn't have done it," Fennimore said again, looking at me and shaking his head.

Okay, okay, I got the message. I wasn't about to hang around here any longer getting dumped on. It wasn't my fault if Fennimore would rather have a best friend who spit and cackled like a goose than one who would sacrifice his own head of hair for him. Some great plan I'd come up with.

I ran and got on my bike, and pedaled home as fast as I could. I hated that stupid George from Pigeon Forge. And I hated Fennimore, too, for not understanding that a person who would do what I'd done for him was the kind of person anybody ought to realize would make a great friend.

My mother was in the kitchen cutting up cheese when I got home.

"So what did Fennimore say about your

haircut?" she asked. "I'll bet he was impressed."

"Oh yeah. Impressed with what a jerk I am."

"Well, I'm sure he'll come around. I think it was very noble of you."

"Mom, can I ask you something?" I said.

"Ask away," she said.

"What does 'The apple doesn't fall far from the tree' mean?"

"It means that people tend to be like their parents. An apple tree produces apples. The parents are the trees, and their children are the apples they produce. Get it?"

I got it all right. What it meant was that no matter what I did, people were always going judge me by the tree I'd fallen out of. Just like Fennimore had done.

"Guysie, which do you think is more festive, white cheese or yellow cheese?" my mother asked.

Why did my tree have to be so weird? Why did my mother have to ask questions about cheese? How was anyone supposed to ever be able to see who I really was? How was I even supposed to know who I was? Maybe I really was weird, and just didn't know it.

"Oh, by the way," my mother said, "Mrs. Adams called a little while ago. Seems they've got a houseguest this weekend. George, I think she said his name was. Anyway, he'll be joining us for dinner tomorrow night."

I'd forgotten all about the dinner! Maybe if Fennimore had been coming on his own, we would have found a way to talk. I could have convinced him that I wasn't a nut like my parents and that he ought to give me another chance. But with George there making fun of me, things between Fennimore and me were just going to get worse.

"This is going to be such fun!" my mother said, happily chopping away. "Assorted cheeses and new friends. What could be more perfect?"

I just looked at her and sighed. I knew there was no point in even trying to explain how much I wished at that moment that my apple had fallen a million miles away from her tree.

Chapter Eleven

The doorbell rang at six o' clock on the dot.

"Come in, come in, you're right on time. Let the party begin!" Mom sang to our company. "Guy! Company's here!"

I came out of my room and stood at the top of the stairs looking down. When I saw what my mother was wearing, I could have kicked myself for not thinking to check on her beforehand.

She had on one of what she calls her "hostess-with-the-mostest outfits." This one was particularly bizarre. She was wearing a skirt made out of potholders she'd sewn together. The matching blouse had red flames painted on the front and wooden kitchen matches hot-glued to the back that spelled out "Too hot to handle." My father was wearing his usual too-short pants, white socks and loafers, and a shirt that matched my mother's. On the back of his, the matches spelled out "Light my fire."

I saw George poke Fennimore in the ribs and point at my father's socks when his back was turned. Fennimore whispered something in George's ear, and they both laughed.

"Why don't you two boys run upstairs and find Guysie," my mother suggested.

"Yeah," said George. "Let's go find Guysie."

Quickly I went back to my room and grabbed a book so they wouldn't know that I'd been standing out there watching them.

"Hey," said Fennimore when they reached my door. "Your mom said we should come find you."

"Here I am. I was just reading," I said.

"Shall we tell Guysie his book's upside down?" George said to Fennimore, giving him another one of those pokes in the ribs.

I blushed and put the book on the night-stand beside my bed.

There's only one chair in my room. It's one of those rolling desk chairs. George sat down in it, leaned back, and put his feet up right on my desk.

"You know who talks about you all the time, Fenn?" George said, ignoring me as though I wasn't even in the room. "Janice Greenhut."

"No way," said Fennimore.

"Who's Janice Greenhut?" I asked, figuring I might as well try to join in the conversation.

"Some girl you don't know," George said dismissively. "Anyway, she's pining for you big-time, Fenn. I swear. Remember that valentine she sent you last year?"

"That was gross," Fennimore said.

"Be Mine, Sweet Valentine and I Shall Be Thine," they recited in unison. Then they both laughed and pretended to gag.

"Oh, remember Kyle Kibble?" George

went on. "He broke his ankle skateboarding, and now he's got pins in it. He can put refrigerator magnets right on his skin, and they stick to him."

"I never broke a bone," I said, making another attempt to join the conversation. "But I know this kid, Bob-o Smith, who got a peanut stuck up his nose and had to go to the hospital to have it taken out."

"Really?" Fennimore said.

"So what?" George jumped in, grabbing Fennimore's attention back with both hands. "Remember that time we went to the ball game and we saw that guy hurling over the railing onto the hot-dog vender?"

Another fit of laughter as Fennimore and his best friend, George from Pigeon Forge, recalled yet another wonderful, perfect, terrific time they'd spent together. I gave up trying to be a part of the conversation. They didn't seem to notice. For the next forty-five minutes they talked about people I didn't know and events I hadn't been a part of. I might as well have been a dust bunny under the bed for all they cared.

My mother called us down to dinner. I kind of wanted to sit by Fennimore, but George elbowed me out of the way and plopped himself down next to him. They whispered and giggled together through the whole meal.

I'm not even going to go into the gory details of what the fondue was like. Let's just say that festive and interactive didn't begin to describe it. Lumpy and disgusting is a lot closer. When it was finally over and they'd all gone home, I was in as foul a mood as I'd ever been in.

"I like your friend Fennimore," my father said as he scrubbed a plate and handed it to my mother to dry.

"In case you didn't notice, he's not my friend," I said. "He's George's."

"Well, I think the two of you looked pretty doggone adorable with those matching buzz cuts. I have to say, Guysie, yours is beginning to grow on me a little," my mother said, obviously trying to cheer me up.

I grunted and rolled my eyes.

"I have a feeling what Guy's hoping is that it will grow on *him*," my father said. "The sooner the better. Am I right, Guychik?"

I nodded glumly. I couldn't believe I'd cut off my hair. For what? Fennimore couldn't care less about being friends with me. Why should he, when he and George had so much in common?

"You were pretty quiet tonight," my mother said as she put away the stack of plates she'd just dried. "Are you and Fennimore still working things out?"

"Mom, leave it alone, will you? There's nothing for Fennimore and me to work out, okay? He hates me. The end."

I sat down at the kitchen table and rested my head on my arms.

"Why do you say that, Guysie?" my mother asked, putting down her dish towel and coming over to sit beside me. "You two will work it out. After all, he came to dinner here tonight. That's got to mean something, right?"

"Yeah, he came to dinner with his best friend, and they both ignored and insulted me all night. That's gotta mean something too, doesn't it?"

"Social triangles can be deadly," my mother said, giving my knee a little pat. "But tomorrow George goes back to Pigeon Forge, and you'll have Fennimore all to yourself again. The two of you will be like two peas in a pod—which reminds me, tomorrow is our first costume fitting for the play, so I'll be coming to school in the morning."

Could my life get any worse? Fennimore hated my guts, Kevin Brudhauser was going to go nuts when he got a load of my haircut, and now on top of that I could look forward to my mother being on display in front of the whole class.

"Why me?" I muttered as I got up and headed up to my room. *Why me?*

Chapter Twelve

As soon as Kevin Brudhauser saw me the next morning, he got hysterical. Every time he looked at me, he'd burst out laughing that stupid donkey honk of his. He didn't make one plucked-chicken crack about Fennimore. Clearly I was the only game in town now.

My mother got there around ten o'clock. I'd made her take off the first outfit she'd put on that morning—a suede jumpsuit with tea bags sewn along the seams like cowboy fringe—and convinced her to wear jeans and a plain T-shirt of my father's (all of hers are decorated). But dressing her normally didn't guarantee anything about the way she was going to behave.

Mrs. Hunn had cleared out a supply closet that would serve as my mother's headquarters, and one by one the kids went in to have their first costume fitting.

"I'm not doing it!" I heard Lana Zuckerman yell when it was her turn to be fitted. "I'm a queen, not a plumber."

It seemed my mother's idea of a queen's scepter was a plunger, the kind you use to unplug toilets and sinks, covered in aluminum foil. King Kevin was similarly displeased with his costume.

"What's this weird bent-looking thing stuck to the front of my crown?" he asked.

I knew what it was. I'd recognized it right away when I'd seen the crown set out on the table that morning at breakfast. It was one of my great-grandmother's sterling silver salad forks, which my dad had accidentally ground up in the disposal a few years ago. My mother cried when it happened, but she managed to cheer herself up by declaring that someday she'd find a way to put it to good use. Apparently that day had come.

When it came time for the shrubs to be fitted for their costumes, I was filled with a sense of dread. What were Fennimore and the other guys going to do when my mother tried to get them to dress up in Astroturf and bathing caps?

"Calling all shrubbery!" she cried.

We followed her into her room. On the table she'd laid out the capes and caps and six pairs of bright-green boxer shorts decorated with shamrocks.

"Mom, do you expect us to wear underwear onstage?" I asked in horror when I saw them. "In front of everybody?"

"It's not underwear, Guysie, it's a costume."

"Looks like underwear to me," said Max.

"St. Patrick's Day underwear to be exact," added Greg.

"I think they're perfect," my mother said. "Clover is vegetation just like shrubs are. And besides that, they were half price at

Finnigan's, since they're left over from last season."

"Gee, I wonder why," grumbled Alex.

"Do you think it might have something to do with the fact that nobody would be caught dead wearing them?" said Henry.

"Uh, duh," said Greg.

Fennimore said nothing.

We all tried on the capes and bathing caps and reluctantly slipped the shamrock boxers over our jeans. You've never seen a sadder bunch of bushes in your life.

"Perfect!" my mother pronounced with satisfaction. "All we need is a little green greasepaint for your hands and faces."

My mom went to get some safety pins from the office to help tighten up Alex's boxers, which kept falling down. As soon as she left, the other shrubs turned to me. Or rather, on me.

"Strang, you've got to do something about your mother. If we go out onstage dressed in these outfits, we're never going to live it down. Brudhauser will torture us for the rest of our lives," Max said.

"Yeah, Strang—you may not mind looking like a geek, but we don't want to," said Greg.

"We're wasting our time talking to him about this," said Henry, jerking his thumb toward me. "Look at him; he's as weird as she is."

"Good point. Strang and his mom already messed up poor Fennimore here. Let's get out of here before she does the same to us. Come on, Fennimore—you've suffered enough."

The five of them took off their costumes and went back to the classroom, leaving me behind. It was so unfair. *My* haircut made me a geek, but *Fennimore*'s haircut made him "poor Fennimore," just another sorry victim of those horrible Strangs. My mother returned a minute later with the safety pins.

"What's the matter? Where is everyone?" she asked when she saw the look on my face.

"Where does it look like they are? They're gone, Mom."

"To the bathroom, you mean?" she asked.

"No. They left for good."

"Why on earth would they do that?"

"Why? Because they're afraid of us, that's why. They think we're weird. And you know what? They're right."

"Oh, pooh. I know people think I'm a little left of center, but you? You're as normal as apple pie, sweet pleat."

"Yeah, but don't forget where the apples for that pie came from," I said. "Face it, I'm doomed for life, Mom. Doomed and bald."

"You're not bald," said a familiar twangy voice behind me. "Besides, according to this fashion magazine my mama showed me last night, the buzz cut is back. We're not dweebs—we're hip, Guy. And you know what? So are these wild costumes, if you ask me."

I turned around and watched in amazement as Fennimore walked over to the pile of costumes on the table and pulled on a cape and bathing cap. "How do I look?" he asked my mother.

She adjusted his cape a little and pulled the cap down lower on his forehead.

He looked ridiculous.

"Perfect," she said. Then she handed him a pair of boxer shorts. He started to put them on, but then he stopped. "Mrs. Strang," he said, "you're the boss. So if you tell us that shrubs have to wear green underwear onstage, I'll do it, and I think Guy will go along with that too. Right, Guy?"

He looked at me. I shrugged, and he continued. "But if you ask me, I don't think the rest of those guys are going to go along with it. That means Guy and I would be the only shrubs."

"That would be a shame," my mother said, sadly surveying the pile of costumes she'd worked so hard on.

"But I have a suggestion," Fennimore went on. "Instead of boxers, what do you think of green *sweatpants?*"

"Hey, that's a great idea!" I said.

"What do you think, Mrs. Strang?" asked Fennimore.

My mom looked at Fennimore and smiled. Then she ran her hand gently over the top of his fuzzy head.

"I think green sweatpants are wonderful," she said. "And so, Fennimore Adams, are you."

Chapter Thirteen

A loud bang made me jump. It was the double doors of the emergency room swinging open. A nurse pushed a hospital gurney out of the room. Buzz was lying on it, looking pale and still, and Mrs. and Mr. Adams were walking next to it.

"Is he okay?" I asked, jumping up and running over to them. "Is he okay?"

Buzz looked awful. Tubes were running up his nose, and there were needles taped to the backs of his hands. Some sort of machine beeped and hissed, and bags of clear liquid hung from poles on both sides of the gurney. At first I thought his eyes were shut, but then I saw that they were open just a slit, and I could see them moving back and forth.

"He's awake!" I cried. "Look, Mom, he's awake. Buzz, can you hear me? Buddy, it's Guy. Can you hear me?"

"They're taking him to surgery," Mr. Adams said quietly, putting his hand on my arm and pulling me away as the nurse continued down the hall with Buzz.

"Surgery?" my mother said, coming over and putting her arm around Buzz's mom.

"Some of his ribs were broken by the impact, Lorraine, and there's internal bleeding," she said. "They said there's no guarantee. Can you believe that's what they said about my child? There's no guarantee." Then she began to sob, and Mr. Adams took her away down the hall to try to calm her down. The fact that she was still wearing the Mother's Day apron just made the whole thing even sadder somehow.

"Mom, what does it mean?" I said. "What's happening?"

"It's too early to tell," she told me.

"Do you mean too early to tell what's wrong, or too early to tell if he's going to be okay?"

"It's just too early to tell, Guysie," she said. "Listen, baby, I need to call Jerry and fill him in. And I'm going to try to reach your dad too. He's probably midair somewhere between San Diego and here, but I'll leave him a message on his cell. Wait for me here, okay? If there's any change, come find me downstairs."

She went off to find a phone, leaving me by myself. I counted the tiles from one side of the waiting room to the other. I pulled on my eyebrows and blew wishes for Buzz as the second hand traveled impossibly slow circles around the clock. Finally I closed my eyes, willing myself back into the only safe place Buzz and I could be together.

Chapter Fourteen

We rehearsed the play for about two weeks. During that time my mother came and went, causing a stir whenever she appeared with some new ridiculous thing she expected someone to wear.

"Princesses are supposed to be pretty, you know," the girlie-girls complained when she showed up with dresses she'd made for them out of newspaper and brown twine.

"It's part of the theme," my mother explained. "What appears to be common is in fact extraordinary and vice versa."

There were tears shed and some foot stamping until it was decided that the theme wouldn't be sacrificed if the princesses were allowed to wear nail polish and red lipstick.

Lana's plunger scepter was exchanged for one made from my mother's old twirling baton from high school covered with glitter and topped with a tinfoiled tennis ball. Kevin was too busy making fun of our shrub costumes to make a stink about his crown.

"You look like green boogers," he hooted.

We all agreed that it would have been even worse if we'd been wearing the boxers instead of the sweatpants my mother got for us.

The afternoon of the play everyone was pretty nervous, including my mother.

"I hope the audience will appreciate the underlying message, and not just think I was trying to cut corners by using recylables," she said as she adjusted the paper dresses on the princesses, who had secretly conspired to wear not only nail polish and lipstick for the performance but bright-blue eye shadow, rouge, and a lot of sparkling jewelry as well.

My father came to help out backstage,

which was probably not the best idea in the world. He has bad eyesight, and he can't see very well in the dark.

When the curtain opened, the first thing the audience saw was Lana's scepter flying through the air as my father tripped over her big feet, sending them both sprawling onto the stage.

My mother was on the opposite side of the stage when it happened, and I guess her old reflexes kicked in, because she caught the baton perfectly in midair and, spinning it over her head like a majorette, marched across the stage to help Lana and my father untangle themselves.

And that was only the beginning.

Kevin got a horrible case of stage fright and completely lost his voice. Mrs. Hunn told him to just move his lips, and she asked my father to read his lines loudly from backstage. Because of my dad's poor eyesight and the bad lighting, a lot of King Kevin's lines were a little off.

"My dear queen, however shall our poor son find happiness?" came out as "My dreary queen, however shall our poor son find hamburgers?"

Bob-o didn't miss a single one of his cues, but he would probably have been beheaded anyway for nose picking while on duty.

The biggest surprise was that the shrubs were the absolute hit of the show. The first time we came out in our costumes, the audience broke into spontaneous applause. All that attention ignited the hidden ham in the six of us, and instead of being the quiet little bushes we'd been during rehearsals, we suddenly turned into the dancing, entertaining bushes Mrs. Hunn had so fervently hoped for.

Fennimore was the ringleader. At first I thought he'd lost his mind. He was absolutely outrageous.

"Follow me," he'd whisper at each of our entrances. And that's exactly what we'd do. Follow him around the stage doing whatever he came up with—wiggling our behinds, leaping and spinning, and doing something he later told me his mother had taught him, called the bunny hop.

When the curtain fell to thunderous applause, King Kevin slunk off in embarrassment while Queen Lana fumed. "That moronic audience missed half of my lines, they were so busy being amused by a bunch of hammy little crudballs in bathing caps."

My father whisked my mother away for a celebratory lunch when it was over. I stayed behind for the cast party, and afterward Fennimore and I walked home together.

"Can you believe Brudhauser lost his voice?" I said.

"Forget about him teasing us anymore," Fennimore said. "We've got something good over him now."

"Man oh man, Fennimore, you sure are *funny*," I said.

"Yeah?"

"Definitely. The shrubs would have stunk

without all that stuff you came up with."

"You know, I think your mom might have been right about those green boxer shorts, though. If we'd worn them, we probably would have gotten even more laughs," he said.

"Could be. But Lana would have had a royal cow if we'd been any funnier." I laughed.

"You know what else your mom was right about?" Fennimore said. "This haircut. Believe it or not, I kind of like it now."

"Really?" I said. "I mean, yeah, actually, I guess it does look pretty cool in a way."

"Okay, no offense, but you, on the other hand, look way better with hair," Fennimore said. "Don't you think?"

"Believe me, I'm growing it back as fast as I can," I agreed.

"Hey, you want to come over now and see that blue-footed boobie I was telling you about before?" Fennimore asked when we got to my corner.

"You know there's no such thing," I said. "You just made it up 'cause you like the way it sounds."

"Did not."

"Did so."

"Come on, I'll show you. One thing though. There isn't anything good to eat at my house. No snicker dillies or anything like that."

"Snicker doodles," I corrected.

"Whatever," he said.

Turns out Fennimore was telling the truth about the boobie, and about the snacks too. There was plate of rice cakes waiting on the table when we got there.

"These are only good for one thing," he said, picking up a rice cake. "Watch this."

He held it like a Frisbee and sailed it across the dining room all the way into the living room, where it skidded to a stop on the top shelf of the bookcase.

"Cool," I said.

"Wanna try?" he asked, handing me a

cake. "Ten points for the top shelf, five for any of the others."

I threw it across the room toward the bookcase, but as it sailed through the archway, Fennimore's mother came around the corner and it hit her square in the forehead.

"What in the world!?" she cried out. "Guy, you'll have to forgive me if I lose my temper in front of company now."

I felt my face turning bright red. I was in trouble now.

"Whoops! Sorry about that," Fennimore said quickly, as he got up and retrieved the rice cake. "It was my fault. By accident the little rascal slipped right out of my hand."

"Fennimore Adams, don't you try to fool me. That was no accident. If I've told you once, I've told you a million times not to throw those rice cakes. I certainly appreciated your shenanigans onstage this afternoon, but I won't stand for funny business in my home. Understood?"

"Yes, Ma'am. I'm sorry. It won't happen

again," he said, hanging his head.

Mrs. Adams rubbed her forehead and continued toward the kitchen.

"Fennimore, you didn't have to do that," I said. "I'm the one who hit your mom with the rice cake."

"I know, but I owed you one," he explained.

"What are you talking about?"

"I know you buzzed your head for me," said Fennimore, "That was a pretty cool thing to do, Guy Wire."

Suddenly I felt like I was flying. Had I heard him right? I knew I had. He'd just called me Guy Wire again. A person doesn't take the blame for misfired rice cakes, or call someone by a nickname like that, unless he wants to be your friend. Good friend. Maybe even— But I didn't want to jinx it by saying it, not even to myself.

"Oh, I'm sorry. I forgot, you said you don't really like that name, right?" he said.

"No, actually I like it just fine now," I told him.

"Really? 'Cause I can come up with another one if you want."

"No, it's perfect. And since you gave me a nickname and everything, do you mind if I have for one you too?"

"Depends on what it is," Fennimore said. "I'm not real partial to Southern Fried Chicken Boy, for instance."

"I was thinking since it looks like you're going to be sticking with that haircut, how about Buzz Cut for a nickname? Buzz for short."

He ran his hand over his bristly head. Then he smiled at me.

"Cool," he said.

"Jumbo cool," I added with a big smile of my own.

Chapter Fifteen

"**H**oneylamb? Guysie?"

"Huh?" My head snapped back, and I tried to lift my heavy eyelids. "What's the matter?" I said groggily. "What time is it?"

"It's two in the morning," said my mother.

I rubbed my eyes and looked at her.

"What's going on?" I asked.

"Buzzy's out of surgery, and they say if we're really calm about it, we can see him."

I jumped out of my chair and started talking a mile a minute.

"Is he okay then? Did they say how he is? He's awake? That's a good sign, right? Where is he? Let's go."

"Sweetie pleat, did you hear what I said?"

my mother asked. "If you can be calm, you can see him. Calm. Okay?"

I took a deep breath and exhaled slowly.

"I can be calm," I said.

My neck was stiff from sleeping sideways in the hard plastic chair, and one of my legs was sound asleep, but none of that mattered. I was going to see Buzz.

We took the elevator up to the third floor. Buzz was in the last room on the right. His mom and dad were standing by the bed. His mom was stroking his arm and talking real softly to him. His head was bandaged, and he still had the tubes and needles in him.

"Look who's here, honey. It's Guy. Guy's here to see you."

Buzz turned his head toward me.

"Hey, Buzz," I said.

He didn't say anything at first; he just gave me a look that went right through me. Then he turned his head back and closed his eyes.

"He's not himself yet," Mrs. Adams said. "I'm sure he's glad you're here, Guy."

But I wasn't so sure. That look he'd given me. Was I crazy, or was he trying to tell me he was mad at me? I needed to talk to him alone.

"I know it's a lot to ask," I said, "but could I be alone with Buzz for a minute?"

"I don't know, Guy. He's only been awake for a little while. He's still very weak," said Buzz's mom.

"Please, just for a minute," I asked. "There's something I need to tell him."

Mr. Adams nodded and took Buzz's mom by the arm.

"Come on, Barb, we'll get a coffee down-stairs and come right back. Let the boy have a minute with his friend."

My mother went with them. As soon as the door closed, I went over to the side of the bed.

"Buzz, are you mad at me? 'Cause if you are, I wouldn't blame you. This is all my fault."

Buzz coughed a little, but he didn't open his eyes.

"I'm sorry, Buzz. Sorry for what I did. Sorry for what I said. I don't want you to die. You know that. I would never do anything to hurt you on purpose. I didn't mean to hurt you. You're my best friend, Buzzy. My best friend."

Buzz opened his eyes, moved his head back and forth on the pillow, and groaned a little. Then he held his hand out over the edge of the bed. I thought he wanted me to hold it, which would have meant he forgave me, but when I touched him, he jerked his hand away and started grabbing at the covers and groaning louder.

I ran to the door and started shouting for help. Nurses came running, and then Buzz's parents came back. My mother and I were sent back downstairs to wait.

"Mom, I'm scared," I said.

"I know," she said. "I am too."

Buzz's dad came down later to tell us that they'd taken Buzz back into surgery. There were *complications*, he said. Complications,

and they wouldn't know anything until morning. We should go home, he said.

"I don't want to leave," I told my mother.

"We need to get some sleep, honeybunch. We can come back in the morning,"
she said.

But I refused. My mother called home
and had Jerry bring over our toothbrushes
and a change of clothes, and she stayed with
me that night. She sat in a chair, and I lay
with my head in her lap. She didn't say anything about my tears soaking her skirt; she
just patted my back while I cried. And she
didn't talk about positive energy anymore. I
think we both knew it was too late for that
now. "You can't fight fate," I had said to Buzz.
"It's a losing battle." Whatever was going
to happen to Buzz was going to happen,
whether we wanted it to or not.

Chapter Sixteen

Obviously Buzz's nickname stuck. Not long after I thought it up, everybody was calling him Buzz. Even his own parents. Buzz and I spent a lot of time together, hanging out after school almost every day. I liked him more and more. He was always polite around adults, but around me he was funny and weird in just the kinds of ways I like. His twang got less noticeable over time, and he started calling his mother Mom like the rest of us. Every few weeks he'd call up my mom and make an appointment with her for another haircut. "Maintaining the buzz," they called it.

For a while George's name came up fairly often, and although I never told Buzz, it always made me feel funny when it did. Buzz told me he felt bad about the way they'd acted toward me, but I didn't care anymore; it seemed like ages ago. One day he told me George had written him a letter saying he had a new best friend. I didn't tell him this either, but I was glad.

When school let out, Buzz and I went to work on a project we'd been planning together for months. A fort. We collected all kinds of stuff. We got scrap plywood from under his porch and a bunch of carpet samples from my basement, hauling it all out to a spot we'd picked in the field behind our subdivision. My dad gave us a stack of old records, which we tacked up all over the place as decoration. It wasn't much to look at, but we loved it.

The day we nailed the roof on it, our parents agreed to let us sleep overnight out in the fort. We took sleeping bags, and my mom packed a bunch of food for us, includ-ing a big bag of snicker doodles. Mrs. Adams contributed some juice and a package of rice cakes, which we entertained ourselves with by sailing them across the field.

That night we lay in our fort, swatting mosquitoes and talking in the dark.

"Did you ever think about that question 'Which came first, the chicken or the egg?'" Buzz asked.

"Not really."

"Well, think about it. Which are you— a chicken man or an egg man?"

"Egg, I guess."

"Yeah, me too," he said. "Did you ever think about that question 'How much wood could a woodchuck chuck?'"

"That's not a question," I said. "It's a tongue twister."

"It's both; part tongue twister, part question. So what do you think, how much could he chuck?"

"That depends," I said.

"On what?

"Mostly on what chucking means and

whether or not he can actually do it," I said.

"Why wouldn't he be able to do it?" Buzz asked.

"Well, remember the end of that thing goes: '*if* a woodchuck could chuck wood.' That's a big if," I said.

"You're a big if," said Buzz.

"Oh yeah? Well, you're a big gum wad."

"Takes one to know one," Buzz said.

Two weeks later, on July fourteenth, I turned eight. I had a party. My mother made one of her famous birthday cakes. It had a picture of me on the top, dressed as a shrub. For party favors she gave out the shamrock boxer shorts. We all got silly and wore them on our heads instead of party hats, and Buzz led us around the house in a wild bunny hop that ended with all of us laughing and rolling around on the floor. I wasn't sure what to wish for when I blew out the candles. I came up with something at the last minute though—*Please, let things stay exactly the way they are with Buzz and me.*

When it came time to open presents, I saved Buzz's till last. I don't even remember what it was. But I remember the card. I still I have it stuck to the bulletin board over my desk. There's a picture of a fat, bald baby drinking a bottle on the front, and inside it says, "Happy BURP-day!" It's signed—

> *. . . your best friend,*
> *Buzz*

Chapter Seventeen

After they took Buzz back into surgery, eventually I must have gone to sleep, because when I opened my eyes, bright sunlight was pouring in the window. At some point in the night someone had moved me into another waiting room where there was a couch. My father was sitting in a chair next to me wearing a suit and tie. He'd been away on a business trip all week. It was sort of shocking to see him dressed up like that after having just spent so much time reliving the old days in my head, back before he realized his pants were too short and white socks and loafers looked dorky.

"When did you get here?" I asked, sitting

up and rubbing my eyes.

"Your mom left me a message. I came straight from the airport."

He gave me a big hug and ruffled my hair. I didn't realize until then how much I'd missed him.

"Where's Mom?" I asked, looking around.

"Actually," he said, flashing me a big smile, "she's at home baking a cake."

"What?" I was wide awake now. "Baking a cake?"

"Uh-huh," said my father, "a great big one. It's for a certain somebody who gave us all quite a scare last night but who's going to be just fine now."

I looked at him carefully. "Are you saying what I think you're saying?" I asked.

"Buzz is going to be fine," my father said.

I threw my arms around him and yelped with joy. "You should have woken me up to tell me," I said.

"I didn't see the point. Buzz is still sleeping and probably will be for a while."

Suddenly it dawned on me why my mother was baking a cake. It was Buzz's birthday. It seemed like a million years ago that he and I had been riding along talking about fate and birthday wishes, but in fact it had been only the day before. My head felt tired from the journey backward, but my heart felt full and grateful for the happy place where I'd finally arrived. Buzz was going to be okay.

Mr. and Mrs. Adams said it was okay for me to wait in Buzz's room until he woke up. Finally around noon he began to stir and blink his eyes. His mother stood over him, helping him sip water through a straw and wiping his face with a wet washcloth. I held my breath and waited for him to notice me there. Would he look through me again? Was he still mad at me for all the trouble I'd caused?

It took him a while to see me, but when he did—he smiled. It was one of the most beautiful things I'd ever seen in my life.

"Hey, Guy Wire," he said weakly.

I couldn't help it. I burst right into tears in front of everybody, blubbering like a big baby.

"Sheesh," I heard him say, and that just made me cry harder.

Mrs. Adams gave me a tissue, and after a few minutes I got myself under control. Over the next hour Buzz seemed to get stronger, and pretty soon he even began to sound like his old self. Mrs. and Mr. Adams went home to shower and change, saying they'd be right back. I was glad for the time alone with Buzz.

"Do you remember me coming in here to talk to you before, Buzzard?" I asked.

"No, did I say something I shouldn't have? I was pretty out of it, I think."

"You didn't say anything. You just looked mad. And I don't blame you if you're still mad."

"Mad? About what?" he asked.

"The accident. Remember? I told you about the wish and then—you got hit. This is all my fault."

"You don't really believe in that wish bunk, do you?"

"Yes," I said seriously, "I do."

"Well, go ahead and believe in the Tooth Fairy too if you want, but this wasn't your fault. I wasn't looking where I was going."

"I told you to prepare to die," I said, my eyes welling up with tears again.

"I never listen to what you say. Don't you know that yet?" Buzz said, "Hey, why are you bawling? Does your face hurt or something?" he asked me seriously.

"No, why?" I asked, quickly putting my hands on my cheeks to check.

"'Cause it's killing me!"

He laughed, and so did I.

Then Buzz closed his eyes and kind of drifted off for a minute. When he opened his eyes, he looked kind of worried.

"What's the matter?" I asked nervously. "Do you need me to call the nurse?"

"No, I'm fine. I'm just remembering something. While I was out of it, I think I had a long dream," he said, "a weird one. Like in *The Wizard of Oz*, you know? All these people I knew were in it, only they were different. It was like pieces of the past were flying around in a sort of tornado, and you know who was in it? Mrs. Hunn. She was ringing that little bell she used to keep on her desk. Remember that thing?"

This was too weird. Had it worked? Had my thoughts really reached Buzz somehow? Why else would he have been thinking about Mrs. Hunn, of all people? What if he'd gone along with me on that journey back to the beginning of our friendship? Had he felt what I was feeling? Been able to read all my thoughts? Suddenly something awful occurred to me.

"Was I in your dream, Buzzard? You know, with that weird buzz cut I got after you got yours? And were the shamrock boxer shorts in it, and George and the fort and flying rice cakes?" I asked anxiously.

"*Rice cakes?* I said it was a dream,

goofus, not a nightmare."

"You have to tell me, Buzz. It's important—do you remember anything about—"

But I was interrupted by a tap at the
door. A hand reached in and flipped the light
switch off.

"Hey, what's going on?" Buzz said.

The door swung open, and there were
my mom and dad and Jerry and Buzz's parents. My mom was holding a big cake with
candles on top. They weren't lit, but Mr.
Adams had a flashlight pointed at it, and they
were all singing "Happy Birthday."

"I totally forgot," Buzz said, trying to
scooch up a little so he could see better.

Buzz's mom hurried over to fluff up the
pillows behind him, while his dad raised the
head of the bed so he could sit up. My
mother had outdone herself with the cake.
There was a very realistic version of Buzz on
top, with little yellow candy sticks poking up
for his hair, and mini chocolate chips for
freckles.

"Make a wish, Buzzy," said my mom.

"Actually, I wasn't planning to do that this year," Buzz said.

"Do it," I said firmly. "And make it a good one."

"Okay, fine. I'll do it for you. But in case you haven't noticed, these candles aren't lit."

"Hospital rules," Mr. Adams said. "You'll have to pretend."

Buzz closed his eyes and blew across the candles. My mom cut the cake, and everybody had a piece, except Buzz, who was allowed only Jell-O. And me. I was too nervous to eat.

"I need to ask you something, Buzz. Something important," I said quietly. "In your dream, the one you had after you got hit, did you happen to overhear me talking about a birthday wish I made?"

"You're scaring me here, Guy. You told me about that dumb wish you made right before the accident, remember?"

"Yeah, I know, but this is a different wish

I'm talking about. That was my seventh birthday when I wished for a best friend. I'm talking about my *eighth* birthday wish. Did you overhear it in your dream?"

Please. I thought. Make him not have heard the wish I made—*Let things stay exactly the way they are with Buzz and me.*

"I swear on my mother's spit I do not know what you wished for on your eighth birthday," Buzz said, holding his hand over his heart. "Satisfied?"

"Yes," I said with great relief. "'Cause that means even though the first wish came undone, the second one has kicked in, which means we're safe."

Buzz looked at me.

"Don't leave me hanging here, tuna brain. What was the wish?"

"Are you nuts?" I said. "Fate doesn't go around handing out second chances every day, you know. I'm never, *ever* telling you what that wish was, got it?"

"Suit yourself, toe jam," Buzz said.

"I will, hangnail."

"Monkey rump," he said, grinning at me.

"Takes one to know one," I shot back.

"Okay boys, that's enough now." Mrs. Adams laughed. "Buzz needs his rest now."

"Thanks for the cake, Mrs. Strang," Buzz said.

My mother came over and kissed Buzz on the top of his head.

"You're welcome, Buzzy. I promise to make you another one when you're well enough to actually eat it."

Visiting hours were over. A nurse came in and tried to hurry us out. Buzz offered her a piece of his cake and then laid a little of his old southern drawl on her. It charmed her like a snake, and she let us stay a little longer.

When it was finally time to go, I looked at my best friend and smiled.

"See you tomorrow, Guy Wire," he said.

"Yeah," I said. "See you tomorrow."